To Margaret Grieco–
A fantastic friend who is a kindred spirit of
Dolley Madison

* Note to readers: The term "red skins" as used to describe Native American Indians was a part of everyday speech in 1812. Today that phrase is considered offensive. In my use of those words in this story, no slight or injury was intended to those of Native American descent. I used the words to remain true to the historical speech of the times.

The Silver Suspect

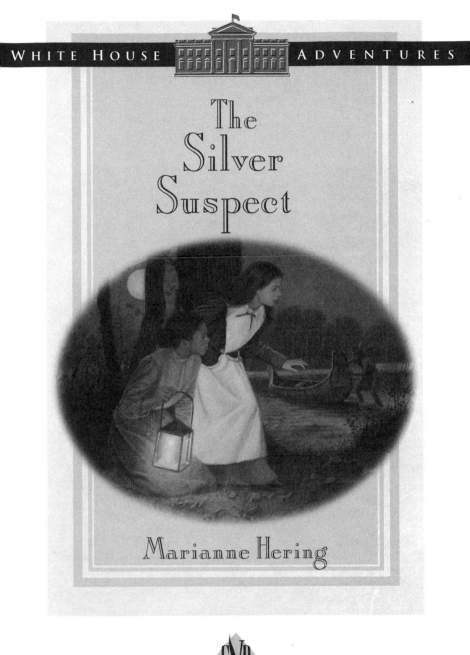

Marianne Hering

Chariot Victor Publishing
A Division of Cook Communications

Chariot Victor Publishing
A division of Cook Communications, Colorado Springs, Colorado 80918
Cook Communications, Paris, Ontario
Kingsway Communications, Eastbourne, England

THE SILVER SUSPECT
© 1999 by Marianne Hering

Edited by Kathy Davis
Designed by Thomason Design Center
Cover illustration by Matthew Archambault

First printing, 1999
Printed in the United States of America
03 02 01 00 99   5 4 3 2 1

Library of Congress Cataloging-in-Publication Data

Hering, Marianne.
    The Silver Suspect / by Marianne Hering.
       p.   cm. – (White House adventures ; 3)
    Summary: Having come to Washington City to visit her aunt, Dolley Madison,
eleven-year-old Annie encounters a mystery involving the disappearance of things from
the White House.
    ISBN 0-7814-3066-6
    1. Madison, Dolley, 1768-1849—Juvenile fiction.   [1. Madison,
Dolley, 1768-1849—Fiction. 2. White House (Washington, D.C.)—Fiction.
3. Mystery and detective stories.] I. Title. II. Series: Hering, Marianne.
White House adventures; 3.
PZ7.H431258Si 1999
[Fic]—dc21   98-54956
                                           CIP
                                           AC

CHAPTER

1

The Spinning Game

The stagecoach suddenly came to a stop, and the six horses pulling it whinnied in protest. Eleven-year-old Annie awoke to the thunder of rifle fire. She threw herself to the floor of the coach to dodge any stray bullets that might come her way.

Two more shots. A pause, then a single blast.

After another pause the stage door flew open, and the driver stood in the doorway. Annie slowly got up off the floor. She sat on the seat and brushed off her plain gray dress. Postal coaches weren't known for their cleanliness.

"Sorry, miss," the driver said. "I had to shoot at a red skin. I didn't mean to scare you—you being a Quaker and all of that."

Annie nodded, knowing that her simple clothes and white bonnet and collar stood for peace and a nonviolent life. The driver had only been doing his job. He wasn't a Quaker and bound by their nonviolent ways.

"Are we there yet?" Annie asked.

"Yes, that's the strangest thing," said the driver
as he took off his black hat and wiped his brow with
a handkerchief. "I wasn't looking for trouble right at
the foot of the President's House. But there he was,
a skinny, black-haired red skin slinking away into the
bushes by the river. If it makes you feel better, I didn't
try to hit him. I was just scaring him off."

Annie forgot about the Indian as soon as she
looked out the stagecoach door and saw the huge
mansion made of grayish white stones. It had a
few small wings next to it, which she found out later
were the carriage house, meat house, and wine cellars,
along with storage areas for coal and wood, and the
servants' privies. But the house stood alone on a hill
surrounded by a low stone wall. Two giant stone
eagles marked the entrance to the front door.

Annie hopped out of the coach. It had been her
home for four days as she traveled from her house
in Virginia to Washington City to visit her uncle and
aunt, James and Dolley Madison.

"Let me help you with your bag," the driver said.
Together they went to the front door of the
President's House.

A well-dressed French doorman took charge of
her. Annie marveled that the buckles on his shoes
were so big and the ruffles at his cuffs so white. She
was used to men who wore only simple clothes. For
Quakers, buttons even had to be sewn on the inside
so they wouldn't shine and be considered vain.

She stood in the vast entryway looking up the long, wide staircase with the curled banister and plush carpets. She had known that President Madison would be busy because of the threat of war. His vice-president, George Clinton, was also gravely ill. But she had expected her aunt, Dolley Madison, to be waiting for her.

The Frenchman left her alone in the family dining room and took her bag with him as he disappeared.

She was all by herself, sitting in a comfortable chair at a huge mahogany table with eight thick legs. She nibbled at the ham, green beans, and buttered rolls that had been set before her by a cheerful servant woman. But it was difficult to eat because she was wondering why her aunt had not come to welcome her.

When she heard the dining-room door open, she put down her fork and looked up, hoping to find Dolley. Instead, Dolley's son was there. Handsome, tall Payne Todd leaned lazily against the doorframe, studying her. She stood and gave her cousin a smile and a small curtsy.

"Well, Annie," he said. "You have grown a bit. But I think I can still play the spinning wheel."

In three long strides, he had picked her up and put her across the back of his shoulders like a fur stole. He twirled around and around so that Annie felt like a weather vane in a hurricane. She wondered that she had ever enjoyed this as a young child.

By the third spin she demanded, "Put me down, Payne Todd!" But her cousin merely laughed. Her stomach lurched when she caught sight of herself in a looking glass. Pictures, shelves with gold statues, and a wooden clock all twirled around. The candlesticks in lamps attached to the walls spun dangerously close. Her head almost knocked one over; she felt her bonnet brush it.

Payne held onto her at her arms and hips and laughed some more. Suddenly a girl's voice cried from the doorway, "Stop! Can't you see she's afire?"

CHAPTER

Aunt Lucy's Wedding

Payne Todd went on laughing and spinning, not heeding the warning of the servant girl. Annie sniffed the air, and then screamed in earnest. From the acrid burning smell, she could tell it was coming from her hair.

Whether from Annie's scream or the smell of smoke, Payne began to slow down. Annie wrestled her top arm free from his hold and managed to throw off her bonnet before he put her down. The white cap landed on the dining table, the flames jumping higher once the cap was off. The housemaid was waiting with a pitcher of water. She poured it right on the bonnet.

"No, Jasmine," Payne snapped. "That water will ruin the wood. Go get a rag to wipe it up."

"Yes, Master Todd," the girl murmured.

The black-skinned girl rushed from the room as Annie hurried to the looking glass. A thatch of her hair had been singed by the burning bonnet. She slapped at the side of her head to put out any of the fire that still could have been burning. Frizzled bits of her black hair stuck out from her head like branches on a winter oak.

She turned to look at her cousin. But she didn't say anything out of anger. She had been trained since birth that Quaker children hold their tongues. Payne took her silence for forgiveness and ruffled her hair. "Nothing but a harmless joke, Annie," he said. "How was I supposed to know your bonnet would catch fire?"

Just before he left he said, "Oh, I have a message from mother. She said to tell you she had to call on a foreign minister's wife. She didn't want to offend her, seeing as how there's probably going to be a war. The government of the United States needs all the friends it can get. You're to make yourself at home."

Then he left, and Annie was alone in the family dining room once more. She stomped her foot on the floor in frustration.

Jasmine crept through the servants' door with a bundle of rags in hand. When she saw that Payne was gone, she got more confident and asked, "Are you all right, miss? Your hair sure looks a fright."

Annie smoothed down her hair again, glad that the Bible says the Lord "looketh on the heart" and not on outward appearances. She nodded to the servant girl, who was staring at her with curiosity in her dark brown eyes.

The servant turned to wipe up the water. Over her shoulder she said to Annie, "You'll get used to his ways. At least that's what my mama says, but I'm not used to Master Todd yet. Don't know if I ever will be."

* * * * *

In 1812 weddings were usually small, simple gatherings because it was too expensive for most guests to travel. Annie had arrived just in time to be at the wedding of another of her aunts, Lucy Washington. Lucy was Dolley's sister.

This event had been organized at the last minute, and it had surprised everyone. But no one was more astonished than the groom. Lucy had rejected him and asked him to leave Washington City days before.

That man was Supreme Court Justice Thomas Todd. When Lucy changed her mind, she sent him a letter asking him to come back. Justice Todd had turned his carriage around and hurried back to his bride-to-be.

The minister leading the ceremony that evening was from St. John's, an important Washington City church. James Madison, the president of the United States, gave the bride away. But even with all those famous people around, it was the president's wife who got most of the attention. Dolley looked like a burst of sunshine in a bright-yellow velvet dress. Her turban had more feathers jutting out than a living peacock. Her jewelry caught the glow of the candlelight from the chandelier. Annie didn't know which sparkled more, the necklace or her aunt's personality.

Annie certainly felt that she didn't look right. She had spent all morning getting ready, worrying about how to wear her hair because she no longer had a bonnet. She decided to wear it plain and long down the back. But as soon as the wedding began, Annie forgot herself and enjoyed the beauty of the service.

After the bride and groom said their vows, the wedding ended and the bridal party broke out of their little cluster around the minister. Payne left the group after he kissed the bride on her cheek. Annie tried to avoid him. She sank down into a large yellow chair near the window, pushing herself deep into the cushions. But Payne saw her and strode to her hiding spot. He looked elegant in his clothes. His breeches were close-fitted and his stockings of the finest silk. The long tails on his jacket made him look tall and thin.

"You can't hide that dull gray dress in such a bright chair," he said. "Couldn't you find something more cheerful to wear, especially to a wedding? You're dressed for a funeral."

"I'm a Quaker," Annie answered quietly. "Quaker girls always wear plain clothes. We're not to look vain. We have an 'Inner Light.'"

"But my mother only wears gray in the mornings now, and she was raised a Quaker," he said. "Maybe you can learn a thing or two from her."

Annie knew she looked dull. It confused her that Aunt Dolley spent so much effort and money on looking wonderful. Annie secretly longed to wear the pretty clothes and jewelry she saw other girls and women wearing. Most of Annie's aunts and uncles had dropped the Quaker ways when her grandfather had died. Even Dolley had left the Quaker society to marry James Madison.

As a result of leaving the Quakers, Dolley Madison had decided to fill her life with color. The rooms of the President's House and Dolley's clothes were bright as the rainbow.

Annie felt like a plain wren in a world of parrots and peacocks. She was embarrassed by Payne's words and could feel her cheeks growing warm. Her expression turned into a frown as she wondered if it was *really* wrong to wear pretty clothes.

"Oh, don't scowl like an old woman choking on a prune pit," Payne said. "I was only joking. Your dress is fine."

Annie again wanted to say something back, but she held her tongue as she had been taught to do. She wanted peace with her cousin, for as the Bible said, "If it be possible, as much as lieth in you, live peaceably with all men."

Jasmine's father, the butler named James Freeman, came to her rescue. The black man pulled Payne aside and began to whisper. Annie caught part of his message: "Something's missing from the carriage house, a silver harness—a wedding gift for the bride. I don't know where else to look. . . ."

The two men left the room with long strides, their haste telling Annie that the matter was very important. She got up from the huge chair and looked out the window. She did not see them enter the carriage house.

Annie didn't know the curtains completely covered her until two women guests sat down on a sofa near her. Too embarrassed to step out and perhaps startle the women, Annie stayed hidden.

But she soon wished she hadn't.

CHAPTER

Jasmine's Trouble

From behind the heavy yellow curtains, Annie first heard the women talk about how handsome Payne Todd was and how beautiful the bride and Dolley were. The whole family, they said, was a handsome group, except Annie.

"Did you see that niece of hers?" one woman said. "What is her name?"

"Annie."

"Did you see that hair and dreadful dress?" the first woman said. "Her hair is as straight as a broomstick. What a shame she hasn't Dolley's curls."

"Well," broke in the second woman, "at the wedding she looked as ill-tempered as a bulldog that had its bone stolen."

Annie hated to listen and she stuck her fingers in her ears. But more gossip sneaked in.

"Such a pity for poor Madison these days," said the first woman.

"What—"

"Oh, you haven't heard? He lost an important letter proving that the British are planning a war. Now that the letter is gone, Madison will never get the anti-war people to agree to his plans to declare war."

The women must have stood and moved off after that, for their voices died away. When Annie dared to peek out from the curtains, she spotted the women near the buffet tables.

Annie patted her hair down to make sure the burned hairs from yesterday weren't sticking up. Then she pushed aside the curtains and stepped out.

After a few minutes, the two women she had overheard came to speak to her. They were older and more stooped than they had appeared from behind the curtains.

After they introduced themselves, the first woman said, "You are such a lovely, sweet girl. I know your aunt is proud to have you here."

Annie almost let her jaw drop open at the compliment. She had just heard the exact opposite. But the second woman shocked her more.

"I think your hair is so lovely," she said, "and your dress is quaint."

At hearing the outright lies, Annie could only nod. She couldn't explain that she knew the women thought she was ugly because she had overheard them. When Annie said nothing, the women must have thought she was unfriendly too. They moved away after giving her a brief nod, and they were not smiling.

What good is a compliment if it is not true? Annie

thought. *They don't know what I'm like on the inside. That's what matters.*

She wanted to leave, but she couldn't pass up the good country food piled high on the sideboards. After eating a bit of chicken and some corn dishes, she stuffed her apron pockets with raisins and nuts and left for the carriage house. She wanted to know if Payne had helped to find the missing harness.

The earthy smell of the carriage house was familiar to her. Horses and other animals were a large part of Annie's farm life. She pushed open the doors. She was about to close the door and leave when she didn't see James Freeman or Payne, but a beautiful horse whinnied. Stepping in to pet the black horse's nose, Annie murmured to her and gave her a handful of raisins. She noted that the horse's tail and mane had been cropped short, then fixed with bows. It made a beautiful sporty look. Annie, though, preferred the long flowing tails of the other horses.

A small noise sounded from back in the stables. At first Annie thought the heavy breathing sounded like a horse just back from a hard run. But Annie knew none of the dozen horses had been worked because everyone was at the wedding. She walked quietly to the back corner of the stables and found Jasmine. The girl was curled up in a ball, her face pushed into her knees, her arms covering her head. She looked as if she was trying to ward off physical blows.

Annie just stared. Then Jasmine sensed her presence and began to calm herself down. When she had been alone, she had allowed her emotions to let go in tears. In front of a relative of the president, however, she would be in control.

"Am I needed at the house?" the housemaid asked.

"I don't think so," Annie said. There was an awkward silence, and Annie said the first words that popped into her head. "Would you like some raisins or nuts?" She held out her hand with the offering.

Jasmine almost smiled at the kind words. But she shook her head.

"All right then," Annie said. "I'm going to ask. What's wrong?"

"Nothing."

It was the answer Annie expected. She didn't like telling her problems to strangers either. But she pressed, "I owe you a favor for helping me stop Payne. I might have burned alive if it weren't for you. Can't I help at all?"

And all of a sudden the story came tumbling from Jasmine, who began to cry again: "Master Todd thinks my papa stole the silver harness! He said that papa must pay for it if they don't find it before tomorrow morning."

"Why does Payne want your father to pay for it? Is it his fault the harness is lost?"

"No, but my papa was the last to see it. He brought it here last night to have ready for the judge and his bride in case they wanted to leave after the wedding."

"Has your father searched the stables? Maybe it's buried under some straw."

"He's cleaned the whole thing. Checked every carriage. It's gone. Someone stole it—but it wasn't my papa."

Annie was silent for a moment. She knew that Jasmine, her mother, and her father were free servants. They could lose their jobs, and the story would be all over Washington City. The Freeman family would have a difficult time getting new jobs.

"Did Payne say how much the harness was worth?"

"No, miss," said Jasmine. "But I imagine it's more than our whole family can earn back in five years. That would mean working every Sunday and Mama taking in extra laundry from around town. And she's already as tired as dirt."

"Well then," said Annie. "There's only one thing to do."

"What?" asked Jasmine, her voice cracking like a snapped violin string.

"Find that harness."

CHAPTER

The Mysterious Indian

Jasmine's family searched the kitchen and the servants' quarters in the basement of the President's House. Annie went back to the Oval Room, where everyone was celebrating the wedding. She may have looked odd to the guests, for instead of talking and eating, she was looking for the harness. That meant opening drawers and peeking inside chests tucked away in corners.

She moved into the dining room, a green room with the portraits of George Washington, Thomas Jefferson, and John Adams staring at her from the walls. She checked in the revolving cupboards and in plant stands. She knew a harness for a carriage was large, especially an ornate one made of silver. It would be heavy. It would make noise when moved.

While everyone was still at the reception, she went upstairs and searched through bedrooms. Three bedroom doors were locked: Payne's, one of the guest's from Kentucky, and the judge's room.

Then she just gave up and sat outside the president's room. Someone would have to be awfully silly to hide stolen goods in the president's bedroom. She did not go in.

Still thinking how big the harness would be, she asked herself where she would hide it. *I wouldn't hide it for long. It is so big and heavy, I would get it away as soon as I could. By horse, carriage, or pay someone else, or* . . . she remembered the river . . . *a boat.*

Running down to the doorman, French John, she asked if any porter had come. He said no, very few people worked on a Sunday, let alone Easter Sunday. Then Annie asked if any of the guests had brought in any unusually large objects, or if their luggage was heavy.

"Well, one of the senator's wives had seventeen hatboxes," he said. "But they were all the right weight for a hat. None were heavier than a loaf of bread."

Thanking him, she ran down to the river. Far down the shore almost covered by some shrubs, Annie found a canoe. It had a large crate in it. She lifted the lid. Underneath an old wool blanket lay the silver harness.

Her heart beat with joy, thudding like a drum in a dance band. *Jasmine's father will not have to pay or lose his job! The bride will have her harness!* Then her thoughts got more serious. *But how to catch the thief?*

First she lifted the harness out of the crate and put in on the shore. Then she put some stones in the crate, trying to put as many as needed to make the same weight as the harness. She put the blanket back inside. If the thief came back, he or she might think the harness was still there. The boat had to float as if it were heavy at one end. The stones wouldn't jingle like the real thing, but it would be good enough.

Next Annie dragged the harness back to the President's House. She feared that it might get scratched because she couldn't keep it off the ground, but she didn't want to take a chance on leaving it. She went the long way around through a nearby orchard. Anyone looking from the windows would have a difficult time spotting her.

She left the harness in the coal cellar. Then she ran inside to share the good news with Jasmine.

She found the Freeman family searching the president's library. The office was filled with rows of books, a desk littered with papers, cabinets, and several chairs. The Freemans all had their heads poked inside the cabinets in the walls.

Annie was practically prancing when she told them that the harness was found. The family hugged each other, and Mr. Freeman gave a long, mighty prayer of thanks to the Lord.

Then the Freemans were full of questions. Where? How? Who? Annie told them the how and where. But she didn't know who. None of them did.

Mr. Freeman said, "Well, I'm going to watch that boat to see who comes and takes it."

"You can't do that," Mrs. Freeman said. "You have duties here. You'll be punished if you leave right now. You've already wasted time by looking for the harness instead of watching the kitchen help."

"We'll all take turns," Annie said. "No one will

miss me tonight. The wedding has everyone so happy and busy."

"But I must tell Master Todd," said James.
"He's planning on causing a big stir, saying I took it."

"Are you sure that's wise?" Annie asked. "Payne could tell anyone about the found harness, and if the thief heard, he wouldn't go near the canoe. In the morning you'll be proved innocent."

"You're right," Mr. Freeman said. "Payne would tell the judge, the judge would tell the bride, the bride would tell Dolley, and so on. Soon the whole city would know the harness wasn't in the canoe. No one would come to the boat. And we do want to catch whoever stole that harness."

Jasmine's mother volunteered to take the first watch. Mr. Freeman went off to the cellar to find a better spot to hide the harness until the morning. Annie asked to go second so that she could sneak out just after bedtime. Jasmine and James would take the night shifts.

At just past nine o'clock, after most everyone else had gone to bed, Annie sneaked out the terrace door and down to the river to find Jasmine's mother. The woman had found a good hiding spot behind an oak tree.

"Evening, miss," whispered Mrs. Freeman. "I haven't seen anything come to the river except a thirsty fox. I hope you have better luck."

Annie crouched for two hours in the shrubs, her legs turning numb, and shooing away flying insects that landed on her face. Then Jasmine came, carrying a blanket and a basket of food—items that Annie had not planned to bring but very much enjoyed.

Sitting for a moment together, watching the moonlight fall on the water, the girls shared some rolls with jelly and a piece of cheese.

Suddenly out of the stillness, they saw something. A man, crouched, came up to the canoe. He climbed in.

Good thing it's dark, thought Annie. *Maybe he won't notice that the harness isn't there anymore.*

After the man pushed the canoe away from shore, the girls looked at each other.

"Did you see what I saw?" asked Jasmine.

"I think so. What did you see?" Annie whispered uncertainly.

"Seeing as how it was dark and everything, and how crouched the man was . . ."

"Go on," said Annie.

"Well, miss," Jasmine said. "If I had to say, whoever it was had a feather on his head."

Annie nodded. She too had thought she had seen dark skin. Long black hair. A headband with a single feather. And she'd heard nothing but the soft step of moccasins when she had been expecting the hard thud of boots.

An Indian had stolen the harness.

CHAPTER

The Tomahawk

The next morning, Annie sat on a stool in her bedroom at the President's House. She stared into a large looking glass. The frame was a shiny gold color with birds and berries carved around the edges. She studied her "new look" of curls circling her head. All her life, she had worn her long, thick, straight hair down her back and underneath her bonnet.

But why shouldn't she want a change? Why shouldn't she dress like Aunt Dolley? She did not want to embarrass the Madisons by looking dull and out-of-fashion. And if she couldn't wear a bright dress or at least a gold bracelet, then curls would have to do.

Her aunt's personal maid, Sukey, was curling Annie's hair for her. Dark, gentle hands released the curls from the hot iron bar. They bounced like huge, black springs. Sukey carefully placed the iron curling clamp back into the fire and began counting to ten. She counted to ten five times to make sure the iron got good and hot. Then she wrapped another portion of Annie's hair around the hot iron rod. After letting it cool and removing the rod, the last curl was finished.

"There, Miss Annie," Sukey said. "Now you'll be ready for the dinner tonight."

Annie liked the curls and the way they bounced on her head. Her hair was as glossy as chocolate. She secretly thought she now looked more like her aunt, who was said to be a beauty.

After thanking the maid, she wandered through the house looking for something to do. Her Aunt Lucy and the judge had left right after breakfast. The other houseguests had left early too. Her Aunt Dolley was out calling on friends, and every man in the house was busy with official business. Even her cousin Payne was hard at work. Jasmine was doing her daily duties, so Annie had absolutely nothing to do.

She wound up on a terrace outside, looking at the Potomac and wondering where the Indian had gone. Had he drifted far, or was he nearby, waiting to come back and take revenge on whoever took the harness out of the canoe?

The waters held no answers, so she walked around the house toward Pennsylvania Avenue to watch the people pass. Perhaps someone would notice her curls. Maybe some people she knew would come to the President's House and she could entertain them since her aunt was out.

After half an hour of tossing rocks from the steps of the mansion, she was about to go inside and read a book. But far off down the avenue she saw a group of

Indians walking toward the President's House. As they neared, Annie counted five Indians in beads and war paint and one military man in U.S. uniform, but also wearing a plain brown frontier hat.

Though she knew it was impolite to stare, Annie studied each Indian as the group came nearer. She wanted to see if she recognized the man who had floated away in the night. Also, she had never seen any braves in war paint before; the dark stripes across the face and chest made a terrible sight. One Indian was covered in bear grease.

As she watched, a fierce-eyed Indian came up to her; he seemed as huge as a bear. He took one of her long, glossy curls and held it between his fingers. Annie didn't flinch as he pulled the curl straight and let it bounce back into shape. She did not like to seem afraid; she had to act strong and courageous.

Then, the Indian let out a shriek louder than a pig caught in a fence. He raised his tomahawk.

Annie caught her breath, but she was too scared to breathe out. *He's going to scalp me for staring!* A scream started to come from deep within her, but then the military man suddenly started to laugh. Annie was sure he did it to distract the Indian holding her hair.

"You're frightening the girl, Red Bear," he said. "Leave her be."

Then the other Indians grunted what sounded like laughs to Annie, and Red Bear slowly lowered his tomahawk.

"We have plenty of enemies to fight without

adding the president's niece to our list," the military man continued. "Let's go seek his council."

As soon as they turned toward the door, Annie sneaked around back through the terraces and into the house. She ran up to her room and lay on her bed for a few minutes, thinking about what to do. Then she got up and went to her washbasin. She lay her hair in the china bowl. She lifted the pitcher and was intending to pour the water over her curls to wash them out, when a kind voice called from the doorway.

"Sukey's feelings will be hurt if you wash them out. She spent all morning on them." It was Aunt Dolley, dressed all in blue, a jewelry box in her hand. Annie put down the pitcher of water and flew into her aunt's open arms.

"Those Indians were going to scalp me!" she said, the fear of the previous night and the tomahawk all pouring out of her at once.

"No, dear," Dolley said. "I was coming up in my carriage and I saw the whole thing. Those Indians are here for a meeting with Madison and are staying for dinner. They have all been around civilized folks long enough to know how afraid we are of the tomahawk. He was just teasing, but he must have liked your hair. It is lovely."

"What trouble my hair has caused," Annie said. "I knew it was wrong to curl my hair."

"No, your curls make you look more of a lady. And that's good. Here, I brought you some pearls to wear. I was thinking of them all day yesterday at the wedding. This is the necklace Madison gave me on our wedding day."

Dolley released her niece and opened the jewelry box. They both peered inside at the white, shiny necklace.

"Only wear it to dinners inside this house," Dolley said. "And bring the pearls back to me every night."

Annie lifted the pearls out and held them up to her neck. She peered into the looking glass. "Do you think people will like me better because of the necklace and the curls?" she asked.

"No, dear," Dolley said, "but they do make you look friendly. You are so serious with a determined look on your face. People who don't know you may think *you* don't like *them*."

Annie nodded, remembering the conversation she had overheard. The words "bulldog" and "ill-tempered" lingered in her mind. She didn't want to embarrass her aunt again. She turned around, holding the pearls in her hands.

"Who is it that Annie doesn't like?" said a voice from the doorway, "It had better not be me." Payne walked into the bedroom. In one hand he held a flat box. The other hand held a metal ring, which in turn held up a big rounded container with a sheet over it. From underneath the sheet came movement.

"I've two little surprises. One for Annie and one for you, Dear Mother."

Annie thought, *And why for me?*

Just then there was a horrible shriek from inside the covered box.

CHAPTER

Two Red Gifts

"What is that?" asked Dolley.

Payne answered. "Doesn't it sound horrid? I think it sounds like Annie did the other day in the dining room."

"Let me see what's in there," said Dolley.

"Wait. For payment I must have a kiss first," Payne declared with a playful tone. "You may not like it once you see it."

"Well, if you must have one," answered Dolley, always looking for a way to show affection to her now-grown son.

She gave him a warm kiss on the cheek, following it with a tight hug. "I just love surprises," she said.

Annie wasn't sure that all surprises from Payne would be so wonderful, but she had a good feeling about these gifts.

Her aunt lifted the cloth covering from the larger gift and gave a shriek to match the one that had come from inside just moments before.

Even Annie gave a little gasp of surprise, and Payne laughed merrily at their shock and wonder.

"A parrot! I've heard of these!" Dolley cried, putting her hands to her face.

"It's a macaw," Payne explained. "This one came from the coast of South America."

The bird was red with green and yellow on its wings and tail. It stood on a wooden perch about five inches long. Its feet kept moving from side to side in a sort of frantic dance. As it paced, it bobbed its head, keeping one eye on the three larger creatures staring at it.

"I do believe he likes us," said Dolley. "Look at the way he's hopping about. I think he's trying to get out." She bent down and opened the door to the cage.

The macaw hopped to the doorway and let out another shriek. Payne pulled a peanut from his pocket and held it out for the bird. The macaw reached for it with its hooked beak and quickly cracked the shell in half, swallowing the meat of the peanut.

"May I please give it one?" Annie asked, delighted with her aunt's new pet. "I think he's hungry."

Payne reached in his pocket again, and this time he pulled out some corn kernels. He dropped them into Annie's small clean hand, and she held out the yellow treats to the bird.

The beak tickled Annie's palm, and she was half-afraid the bird would nip her skin. But the macaw soon had the corn eaten without hurting Annie. But when he hopped to her shoulder, his claws dug in

tightly, and she flinched at the pinching pain. Dolley
came to Annie's rescue just as the macaw began to flap
its wings. Mrs. Madison held out a fire poker and the
bird hopped to what it thought an oversized perch.
Dolley carried the bird back to the cage and slid it
inside. The bird gave only a small screech of protest.

Dolley put her hands on her hips and smiled at
Payne. "He's absolutely wonderful, dear. I can't wait
to see what's in the other package."

With all the excitement about the macaw, Annie
had forgotten about the flat box. They all turned to
it then, and Payne picked it up from her bed.

"I won't even charge you a kiss for this," he said,
holding the gift out to Annie.

Annie accepted the gift and lifted the lid from the
sturdy box. Inside was something almost as bright as
the macaw. She held up a red dress with yellow ribbons.
It was the most beautiful dress she had ever seen.
Her mind raced as she thought of reasons to refuse
the beautiful gift. She didn't think her parents would
mind her wearing the dress at the President's House
if it made Dolley happy. And wasn't it all right to
accept gifts from family members? She wanted to
keep peace. To refuse would be rude.

"But I can't wear something this nice," she finally
said. "It's so expensive. What if I ruin it?"

Dolley spoke up for her son, saying, "He earns
a good wage for being Madison's secretary. He can
spend his money as he chooses. And you'll not ruin it.
You can save the dress for dinners and parties. It'll

look lovely with your dark hair and pink skin."

Annie stared at the pretty dress. She plucked at the material with her fingers. She did not want to fight with Payne. She wanted peace. "Thank you, Payne," she finally managed to say, but she didn't give him a kiss. She was grateful for the gift, but not sure how to show it. She was still unsure if she should even wear the dress.

But as Dolley and Payne left with the macaw, Annie held up the red gown and looked at herself in the mirror.

No one will call me a bulldog while I'm wearing this, she reasoned. *I'm going to wear it this very night!*

CHAPTER

Double Indian Trouble

It was at dinner that night that Annie got her first offer of marriage.

A crowd of some twenty Indians and military men gathered for dinner in the formal dining room. Annie recognized the five Indians she had seen that morning, including Red Bear. Annie wore her new crimson dress, pearls, curls, and a smile.

She entered the dining room on Payne's arm, and she thanked him again for the dress. He smiled and said, "I never thought a silly dress could make a girl so different. You don't look yourself."

Annie didn't know how to answer, but she continued to smile.

Inside the dining room, she curtseyed to just about every Indian who entered. Some of them bowed to President Madison and some signaled with their hands. The president wore the plain black homespun clothes that he wore every day. He had worn the same style at his wedding and on the day he was sworn in as president. In snow or sun he wore plain black suits. Annie wondered why he didn't care what he looked like. It was almost shameful that the president of the United States dressed in such shabby, dull clothes.

In contrast, Dolley's turban was coiled in three different shades of green, and it had a forest of blue feathers sticking up from it. The dress matched the feathers and was off her shoulders. Around the bottom was a ruffle of bright green, and the dress swished when she walked. Annie knew that her own dress was brighter in color and that the Indians' war stripes of every color were dramatic, but Dolley's personality and flair brightened her clothes and caused her to sparkle. Annie wondered if an angel in all of God's glory could outshine her aunt.

But Dolley was not to be the woman who got the most attention at dinner that night. Annie had just stuffed a mouthful of corn soufflé into her mouth when the voices at the table began to laugh, and she felt several pairs of eyes upon her. The last time she had paid attention to the grown-ups' talk, it had been about someone in Russia having peace talks.

But something much less serious than war was being discussed, and it was Payne who delighted in telling her.

"Annie," he said, "do you think that seven horses and a dozen goats is enough to buy you for a bride? Or should the president hold out for some guns, too?"

Annie stared at Payne, and then at everyone at the table. The military men and their wives were trying not to laugh out loud. Several had napkins covering their mouths to keep away the giggles. Even President Madison was smiling, and he rarely did so in public gatherings. Her eyes rested on Red Bear. He had the same gleam in his eyes as he did when he had been holding onto her curl. He wanted something.

"What do you mean?" she asked Payne. "Speak plainly, or am I to be the only one who doesn't understand the joke?"

"It's no joke, Annie," the president answered for Payne. "Red Bear wants to buy you as a wife for his son."

"But why?" Annie choked out.

"It makes good sense," the president continued. "You are old enough to marry by Indian standards. Red Bear wants his son to marry into my family. He thinks you are U.S. royalty—like a princess."

"But that's not all," Payne said. "He thinks you are very beautiful and that you look strong. He thinks you will have many sons."

About then, Annie wished Red Bear had scalped her that afternoon. At least that would have been less painful. She felt her cheeks burn hot, and she could tell they were turning as red as her dress. It was embarrassing to think that some strange man was wondering how many children she might have. The praise she was getting for looking nice didn't feel as good as she had expected it to.

She managed a weak smile to Red Bear, who merely grunted back.

"Will someone who speaks his language please tell

him no thank you?"

"But you'd be an Indian princess," Payne teased.
"How can you refuse?"

Then Dolley's voice came from the end of the table. "Don't worry, Annie. We've already explained that you are too young and that you're not royalty. No one will let you be whisked off with the Indians."

Annie, relieved by her aunt's words, went back to eating her dinner. But the food didn't taste quite as good as it had before.

*　*　*　*　*

That night after dinner, Annie had already changed into her nightgown when she remembered that she had to return her aunt's pearls. She placed them gently inside the carved wooden box, took a candle-holder in one hand, and walked down the hall to Dolley's room.

She found her aunt at her dressing table, wiping her face with a white handkerchief.

"You won't tell anyone that I use rouge, will you?" Dolley asked as Annie looked at the red-stained handkerchief. "It's a terrible habit, I know. But I look so old without it, I'm thirty-six, you know."

Annie knew her aunt was forty, but had been lying about her age for so long that just about everyone in the family had forgotten. "I won't tell, Aunt Dolley. I imagine all those other women use it. They also use some stuff to smooth out their wrinkles."

"Well, I won't be using rouge for a while at least. Somehow I've misplaced my last tin of it, and the only stuff I'll use is French. With the trading being cut off, it will be some time before I paint my face again."

Annie smiled at her aunt in the looking glass, putting her hand on Dolley's shoulder. She was about to say something about true beauty coming from within, but her breath was cut off by a sudden fear. Her grip on Dolley's shoulder tightened.

"What is it, dear?" Dolley asked.

Annie made a small motion with her hand to the corner of the looking glass. Then Dolley saw it too.

An Indian wearing war paint was hiding behind the door.

CHAPTER

The Problem with Pearls

Dolley didn't know a word of any Indian language. But she did remember this Indian's name. She stood and turned to greet him.

"Hello, Water Dancer," she said in a formal but friendly tone.

The Indian jumped out from behind the closet door. A knife was poised in the air, ready to strike anyone who came too near.

"Annie," Dolley said in a calm voice, "I need you to go past him and out the door. He didn't hurt you when you came in, and I don't think he means any harm. Madison is still with the generals downstairs; he's too far away to help. Try finding a servant to come quickly."

Walking past the closet door was the scariest trip Annie had ever taken. Barefoot, she took step by quick step. Water Dancer stood still as a mountain; his eyes were the only things moving as he followed Annie's movements.

Once Annie was in the hallway, she took a hasty glance over her shoulder to make sure Water Dancer had not moved. Sure that he had stayed put, Annie sprinted down the twisting servants' stairs. On the way up was Payne Todd.

"Quick," she said to him, "go to Aunt Dolley's room. There's an Indian. He has a knife."

Payne didn't need a second warning. His long legs stretched out, and he took the stairs three at a time. The quickness of his steps spurred Annie on behind him. She thought horrible thoughts all the way there. *Would Water Dancer hurt a woman? Would he harm the president's wife? Would Payne be foolish and fight?*

But when she did arrive, nothing was wrong. Dolley was leading Water Dancer down the stairs by the arm, as if he were escorting her to dinner. Payne was not far behind them saying something in a weird language to Water Dancer. The Indian merely grunted back.

"What happened?" Annie asked Dolley.

"Why, the poor dear was frightened," she said patting his hand. "He lost his way and hid in my closet. He was afraid Madison would be angry at him, so that's why he drew his knife."

"But we are only women. Why was he afraid of us?" Annie asked Dolley, wishing she knew some Indian language so she could talk to Water Dancer.

Dolley just laughed, "He saw me without my rouge, dear. I told you I look dreadfully awful without it."

"Well," Annie said, "I think there have been too

40

many Indians running around the President's House." Suddenly Payne spoke up, "Why do you say that? Have you seen any more Indians about at night?" Annie remembered the Indian that the stagecoach driver had shot at the day she arrived. And last night there was the punt and the Indian she had seen floating down the river. *Does Payne know about that Indian and the harness? Did he see him too?*

Dolley spoke before Annie could reply. "Oh, she's just mad at Red Bear. First he pretended to scalp her, then he wanted to marry her off. She's just not happy today with our red-skinned friends."

The group had made it to the terrace door. Water Dancer pulled away from Dolley once he realized how near freedom was. Suddenly, he bolted out into the night and disappeared.

"That was quick," Dolley said. "Payne would have taken him in a coach wherever he needed to go."

"Maybe he has a boat nearby," Payne said with a quick glance at Annie. She locked eyes with him, but decided to say nothing about the canoe. It would just cause trouble.

The three went back to the family bedrooms. Dolley stopped in the yellow room to say good-night to the macaw and give him a nut. Payne followed Annie up the stairs a little too closely.

"I think that Water Dancer stayed behind to kidnap you," he whispered in Annie's ear. Then he turned and stopped at his door. Taking out a key, he unlocked it and went inside.

"Well, good night," Annie said to his closed door. "Sweet dreams and all that."

She decided Payne had just been teasing and not really trying to frighten her. But it was still difficult for her to fall asleep. Fear of being kidnapped kept her awake until she recalled a comforting Psalm: ". . . hide me under the shadow of thy wings, from the wicked that oppress me, from my deadly enemies who compass me about." Finally, she dozed off to sleep.

She was awakened later by her aunt. Dolley was shaking her arm.

"Annie! Annie! You have to wake up. My pearls are missing. My wedding pearls are gone!"

CHAPTER

The Search

Annie wasn't sure if she was dreaming or not. She had never seen her aunt so upset before. She had also never seen Dolley in a white nightdress, which made her look pale. But her eyes were red and swollen, as if she had been peeling onions. Her voice was high and screechy like a crow's.

"My pearls!" Dolley cried. "Annie tell me that you know where they are."

"Let's think," Annie said, taking her aunt's hand and leading her to sit on the edge of the bed. "I put the box down on your dressing table right before we spotted the Indian behind the door."

"I know. As soon as you left, I got up to talk to Water Dancer. I don't remember much after that except Payne came and started to talk in bits of pieces of some Indian language. Then Water Dancer allowed me to take his arm, and we turned down the hallway to take him out."

"I came back when you weren't but two steps

from your room," Annie said. "But I didn't look in to notice if the jewelry box was still there or not."

Dolley shook her head. "Water Dancer couldn't have taken them, or I would have noticed."

"Maybe you knocked them off the table when you stood up! We should go check," Annie suggested.

Having a plan cheered up Dolley. The two figures in white hurried back to Dolley's room. Since Annie was smaller and younger, it was she who crawled on the floor. She looked for the pearls underneath chairs, the bed, the dressing table, behind the thick orange curtains, and all around the chest of drawers.

Her large brown eyes were almost full of tears when she stood up and faced her aunt. She brushed the dust off of her nightgown and sighed, "Neither the box nor the necklace is here."

"Well, it's a mystery to me," Dolley said, beginning to become her usual calm self. "I'll alert the servants in the morning, and maybe the pearls will turn up somewhere."

For the second time that night, Annie went to bed. This time dreams didn't come so easily. The pretty head on the pillow with the dark curls was full of thoughts about the one person who could have taken the pearls but who had no reason to.

*   *   *   *   *

"I heard about the missing pearls. They don't think you took them, do they?" Jasmine asked the next morning. Her face was scowled with rows on her forehead, like a freshly plowed field.

"No," Annie said. "I'm family. Even though my parents don't have a lot of money, the Madisons know that I would never steal from them."

"Annie, because you found that silver harness for us, my whole family is dedicated to finding those pearls," she said. "If there is anything you want us to do, just let us know. We'll help all we can."

Annie looked at Jasmine. She noted the neat uniform and apron she wore, the white mobcap with the springy black hair underneath. The beautiful dark skin and the honest, bright eyes. But Annie didn't dare to tell Jasmine her thoughts about her cousin in case she was wrong.

Annie said, "The pearls will be easier to hide than that huge harness. We'll have to look carefully everywhere . . . By the way, I haven't asked Payne yet if he saw the pearls. Do you know where he is?"

"He's in with President Madison," Jasmine said. "They're alone."

"All right," Annie nodded. "I'll be waiting for him when he comes out of the president's library."

She hid herself at the bottom of the main staircase of the house behind an umbrella stand and a small table. Three servants passed her on their way, but only one noticed her, Mr. Freeman. But he merely nodded, as if a Quaker girl hiding on the stairwell was as normal as the sun shining.

After what seemed like a hundred years to Annie, but was really only about forty minutes, Payne came out of the library. He did not see Annie, and he turned in the opposite direction and went out on the terrace. Annie decided to follow, but at a distance. She counted to 500 and then followed him. He was tall, and Annie easily spotted his elegant black jacket far off. He was near the east wing, feeding the geese that roamed freely on the grounds.

In order not to be seen, Annie sneaked closer and climbed an oak tree. She made sure she was hidden in a cluster of leaves.

Annie watched as Payne carefully reached into his pants pockets and then held out his palms to the giant birds. Seven gray-headed geese honked and fought each other to thrust their beaks into Payne's hand. Annie couldn't see exactly what they were eating, but she thought it was leftover corn Payne carried for the macaw.

Then Annie realized that something weird was going on. Payne went into a storage room several times. He came out with a knapsack, four large crates, and a hammer. Two by two, he loaded up the geese into the crates and nailed them in. Their long necks stuck out through the slats.

The seventh goose, however, did not want to be caught. Payne chased him around in circles. He tried offering more food, but the bird didn't want any. Finally Payne realized that he had lost when the bird suddenly ran, then awkwardly flew off down the river.

Payne kicked up some dirt, then kicked the last empty crate. The force of the kick sent the crate rolling over four times. He said something out loud, but Annie couldn't tell what it was. From the tone of his voice, she was glad she couldn't understand the words. They probably weren't nice at all.

Then he left. Annie was just about to climb down the tree and follow him, when he suddenly came back.

This time, Payne was leading a horse and wagon filled with bales of hay. First he loaded the crates of birds, and then he moved the hay to keep the crates from sliding. Annie could see he was planning to move the birds, but what she couldn't figure out was *why*.

With Vice President Clinton dying and the country on the brink of war, President Madison needed all the help he could get. He would need Payne as his secretary to write letters. *Why was Payne doing the work a servant should be doing?*

Payne got into the wagon, picked up the reins, and started to move off. Just then, the last goose came back honking, as if daring Payne to chase him again. Payne stopped the wagon just underneath Annie's tree.

He got out and began to lure the bird to him with another handful of corn. While Payne was trying to catch the bird, Annie dropped into the wagon, hiding in between bales of hay.

Before she knew it, Payne was back in the wagon, still without the last goose. Annie was unsure where she was headed. But she was sure that if Payne caught her, it would be worse than when her hair caught on fire.

CHAPTER 10

The Indian Reappears

The ride was long and slow as the horse plodded out of Washington. Annie could tell Payne was heading in the direction of Georgetown, a neighboring city. But because of the gentle rocking of the wagon and Annie's missed sleep from the night before, she quickly fell asleep.

When she awoke, she found herself in the company of a tall, thin Indian. He was standing right next to the wagon on a busy town street.

Annie's heart stopped beating for a second as she took in the reddish skin, the long dark ponytail, and the headband with the single feather. A second later, she realized that the Indian did not know she was in the wagon, and her heart began beating again. But the fear didn't stop. The Indian was bargaining in an Indian dialect with a white businessman. The only words Annie could understand were the ones about money.

She didn't get a good look at the white man's face, but he had on clothes that were much too expensive

for a farmer. He looked like the keeper of a hat shop
or a jewelry store.

The businessman kept on shaking his head. Finally,
the Indian pulled something out of his pocket, Annie
didn't see what, and the businessman's voice changed.
He offered a price that was so high, Annie at first thought
the Indian was selling more than the geese. But the
deal was made, and the Indian took a wad of money.

When the Indian turned to the wagon, Annie flattened
herself as low as possible, trying to meld herself with
the bottom of the wagon. One by one, the Indian hauled
the three crates out of the wagon, and the businessman
stood laughing the whole time. He was enjoying a good
joke that Annie didn't understand, but the Indian
kept silent. Soon he and Annie were on their way.

After about fifteen minutes more of the ride, the
wagon stopped. Annie heard the Indian get off the
driver's seat. She counted to ten thousand, then dared
to lift her head up and peek out. She was at one of the
last places she expected. The horse and wagon were
tied up in front of the Georgetown horseracing track.

But where was Payne?

*　　*　　*　　*　　*

It took Annie about ten minutes to pray up the
courage she needed to act. After asking God for guid-
ance, she jumped out of the wagon. Her first thought
was to find the Indian and see if she could figure out
who he was and what he was up to. Then she decided
the racetrack was a bad place to be. It was one thing
for a Quaker to wear a red dress and pearls, but quite

another to be seen in a place where gambling took place. And by the amount of money the Indian had, she knew he would be gambling for a long time. So she began the long walk home.

From the position of the sun, she could tell that the lunchtime meal had come and gone. Dinner at the President's House was going to be served within an hour. She would not make it home before then, and she would be missed. Her aunt and uncle would send out servants to look for her. How long would it take before anyone thought of heading to Georgetown?

She trudged on toward town. As horses and carriages passed her by on the road, hooves and wheels threw up mud and dirt. Her sensible black shoes were now muddy brown, and her gray dress was splattered with grime. As she neared the main part of town, she wondered if she could get a coachman to take her to the President's House. Surely someone would believe she was the president's niece.

But when she looked down at her filthy clothes and felt her hair all matted with hay, she doubted anyone would believe her.

On she walked, past the general store, the hat shop, a fabric store, and as she walked she marveled at all the things she would never be able to buy as a Quaker. One fine-smelling shop sold only tobacco and pipes. On the outskirts of town there were row upon row of taverns and lodging houses.

She was not in her familiar world. She did not really know the way. Annie prayed for strength.

She heard a horse come up behind her, and it
passed. On its back rode Red Bear. She recognized his
fancy tunic, which was covered in beads and feathers.
About fifteen feet in front of her, his brown horse
suddenly turned and stopped. The Indian stared
at her for what seemed like a hundred years. Annie
saw that glint in his eyes, and she turned to run.

I am not *going to become an Indian princess!*

Before she had moved five or six steps, she heard
the beat of horse hooves. An arm reached down and
plucked her up by the waist. She was put face-down
across Red Bear's legs and the horse galloped away.
After seven or eight seconds, Annie fainted from fear.

*   *   *   *   *

Annie woke up the next morning in her bed at the
President's House.

Am I glad that was all a dream, she thought. But then
she saw her mud-splattered clothes neatly lying on a
chair near her bed. She knew that the geese, the mys-
terious Indian, the racetrack, and the ride with Red
Bear had all happened.

As she stirred, Jasmine came to her side.

"What a day you must have had yesterday,"
she said, her kind face smiling. "Everyone is worried
about you, especially your cousin, Master Todd.
He wants to talk to you as soon as you wake up."

"Why?" asked Annie.

"He didn't tell me," she said.

"Jasmine," Annie whispered, a sudden light burning
in her eye.

"Yes," Jasmine whispered back, feeling the urgency in Annie's voice.

"Go to the carriage house and look for that old wagon. You know, the one that's used to bring things back from market," Annie said. Jasmine nodded.

"Tell me if it's in the carriage house and if there's a knapsack in it. If the knapsack is there, bring it here," she said.

"Why?"

"I can't tell until I know more," she said. "But after what happened yesterday in Georgetown, I have a good guess."

"Is that where you were yesterday—in Georgetown looking for clues?"

"Yes," Annie answered, not wanting to tell the whole story. "And I think I learned about the Indian who took the harness. And about the pearls."

"I almost forgot," Jasmine said as her hands flew to her mouth. "With you missing yesterday and all the fuss—we found the pearls."

"Did you find *all* of them?" Annie asked.

"Well, no," Jasmine said. "We only got back five. Mrs. Madison thinks there were almost seventy on the strand. It's a weird story, but Cook came running to my mother yesterday afternoon. Cook was preparing a goose for a special dinner, and when she cut it open—"

"She found the pearls in its crop," Annie said. Then she turned serious. "Go and find that knapsack, but don't let anyone know I'm awake. I don't want to talk—at least not yet."

CHAPTER

Secret of the Knapsack

When Jasmine came back to the bedroom an hour later, Annie leaped out of bed. "You brought it!" she squealed.

"It wasn't in the wagon, miss," Jasmine explained. "That's why it took me so long. As soon as you said 'knapsack,' I knew what you were looking for. It's a bag that Master Todd takes with him whenever he leaves. It was hidden in his bedroom. By offering to clean all the bedrooms, I got the main housekeeper to loan me her keys. Then I had to make his bed and do the cleaning."

Annie was afraid to open the greenish brown knapsack. She wanted to know the truth, but didn't want to know anything that would hurt Aunt Dolley.

"Well," Jasmine said, holding up the bag. "Aren't you going to see what's in it?"

"You look," said Annie. "Tell me if there's a wig made from horsehair and a large tin of rouge."

The housemaid opened the bag. At first she

frowned, then after rummaging around in it, she said, "They're both there. And the Indian moccasins, the Indian tunic, the Indian headband. Plus a feather."

Annie could tell by the tone of her friend's voice that Jasmine too had figured out that Payne was the Indian who had come to the canoe.

But Jasmine does not know all about the geese Payne sold! And the less Jasmine knew the better for her. The housemaid would probably have to work for Payne for a long time.

Annie pushed the knapsack underneath her bed and hugged her loyal friend. "Thank you," she said. "I never would have dared go into his room. But you mustn't tell anyone about the knapsack."

"But what if he steals again!" Jasmine said, pulling away from Annie. "What if next time we don't find the harness? What if next time my father or my mother or *I* get accused of stealing? We have to stop him."

Annie sighed. "All right. But let me do it. I'm family. They'll believe me. The less said about the Freeman family the better for you and your parents. I don't want Payne knowing that any of you had a part in my scheme to catch him."

Jasmine nodded, heading toward the bedroom door. "God be with you when you tell Mrs. Madison. She's going to raise a ruckus."

But Annie was already thinking, *I'm going to tell someone, but it isn't going to be Aunt Dolley.*

Annie needed courage for her next task. She looked at the dirty Quaker dress and decided it would not do.

She needed to look her best. She washed her face
and hands with the cool water Jasmine had left in
her washbasin. Then she put on the red dress and
pulled her hair back with a yellow ribbon.

She picked up the knapsack and looked in the
mirror. *I'm ready,* she thought, but for some reason
the dress didn't give her the courage she was seeking.
O God, she prayed, *help me to speak the truth, even though
it will hurt people. And please help me remain at peace with
my cousin Payne. I don't want an enemy, but he must
be stopped.*

It was tricky for Annie to go downstairs without
being seen. For one reason, the dress was so bright
it was difficult to hide. For another, Aunt Dolley and
Payne were waiting to find out what had happened
to her yesterday. They would come rushing to her if
they saw her. No doubt Red Bear's account when he
brought her home had caused some alarm. Dolley would
have been worried about her safety. Payne would
have been worried that she saw him in Georgetown
dressed as an Indian.

But she finally made it downstairs and into the
president's library. Because she couldn't take the risk
of being seen in the hallway, she didn't knock on the
door. Annie walked right in. At first President Madison
didn't look up. But when she stood right in front of
his desk and gave a little cough, he glanced up from
his papers. He looked startled as if seeing an oak tree
sprout up in the center of the room.

"Well, Miss Annie Payne," he said, "to what do I

owe the honor of this visit? You haven't changed your
mind about marrying Red Bear's son?"

"Oh, no!" Annie cried before she could tell that
her uncle was teasing. When she looked carefully at
his face, she could see how tired he was even though
there was a friendly twinkle in his eye. *He hasn't gone
to sleep in days, I bet. He's so worried about war all he does
is work and write letters.*

"Well then, please sit down," he said, standing
and moving away from his desk. He pushed a little
chair with green cushions right next to his desk and
motioned for her to sit down. As they stood next to
each other, Annie realized that he was only a few
inches taller than she was. But she sat down quickly
and plopped the knapsack at his feet.

"It's a long story," she said. "And I don't think
you'll like the ending. And I want to keep it a secret."

"Let the truth do its worst so that it then can do
its best," he said.

So Annie began her story. It began with the search
for the harness and seeing the Indian come back to
the canoe.

Next she told about the night the pearls were
missing and how Dolley mentioned that her rouge
was also gone. When she got to the part where she
spied on Payne and dropped into the wagon, she had
to look at the flowered needlepoint carpet. She was a
little ashamed at thinking badly of her cousin. But the
president didn't seem to think it was so wrong. He
had a lot of questions about the geese.

"You saw him feeding Dolley's pearls to the geese?" he asked.

"Well, no," she explained. "I think it was corn and pearls, but I can't be sure. You know geese eat small rocks to aid their digestion?"

"I've been a farmer all my life," he answered Annie, "and yes, I have noticed that geese and ducks and chickens need grit in their diet."

"So," Annie hurried on, "one of the geese got away and he put the rest in the wagon. I sneaked in when he wasn't looking."

"Then what happened?"

"I don't remember, because I fell asleep in the wagon," she said. "But when I woke up, I was on the main street of Georgetown, and a tall, skinny Indian with long thick hair and rosy red skin was selling the geese to a businessman."

"Did they speak English?" the president asked.

"Not exactly," Annie said. "But I understood them when they mentioned silver."

"How much did the Indian sell the geese for?"

When Annie named the sum, the president clapped his hands. "Well, the pearls were worth a bit more than that," he said, "but it was a good price seeing that the pearls were in such an interesting package."

Annie finished her story, telling about the racetrack and her walk home, and finally about Red Bear carrying her off. She hadn't realized she had been talking so fast that she was out of breath. President Madison got up and gave her a glass of water. The he sat down and thought. As he stared into space, thinking about her story, Annie studied him carefully.

The worn black suit was comforting to her now, and she noticed that his round, homely face had lines of wisdom etched in it. She wondered that she had ever thought him shabby. He was a man with more important things to do than worry about clothes.

Suddenly he spoke. "Do you have any proof?"

Annie was ready for this. "There are the pearls that cook found in the crop of the last goose," said Annie. "That proves the geese were fed the pearls. And then, there's this." She picked up the knapsack and gave it to her uncle.

After he looked inside he said, "That is Dolley's rouge. I've seen tins like this on her dressing table before. And this wig is made from horsehair. No doubt it's from the black mare that Payne owns. I wondered why he cut her tail."

"What are you going to do?" Annie wondered aloud. She hadn't realized she'd spoken until the president looked at her with a quick glance.

"I've decided to tell you a secret in return. And then I will tell you what I am going to do."

Annie's eyes opened as wide as sunnyside up eggs.

"Last month an important letter was stolen from this office," he began.

Annie gasped, half-afraid that Payne had taken it.

The president continued, "Some friends of mine informed me that it was sold to a British minister by an Indian. They described the Indian as almost being sunburned, he was so red."

Annie's eyebrows raised in shock. *Payne stole important papers from the president!*

"I have also heard that Payne is at the racetrack in Georgetown almost every week, and that he owes a fair sum of money. I pay him a lot, but he gambles the money away... And now, this is what I am going to do."

Annie closed her eyes. When he told her his plan, she was so happy she jumped up and gave him a hug and a kiss.

President Madison smiled and said, "You are a very smart, good, and brave girl, Annie. Those Quakers raise good women. I should know. I married one."

CHAPTER

A Trip Abroad

Annie left the president's library thinking about the compliment he had just given her. It was the first one she had gotten about what she was like on the inside, and it felt a lot nicer than someone telling her that she had pretty hair or a nice dress. *I really shouldn't worry about my outward appearance so much*, Annie thought. *If the president and God notice my heart, then that's what I'm going to work on.*

As she passed outside the oval room, the macaw gave a shriek. Annie caught sight of herself in a large looking glass in the hallway. A twisted gold-colored candelabra cast it's light upon her, and she frowned. *This dress is too red. I look like a silly parrot. I may as well shriek for attention as wear this dress.*

She ran upstairs to her bedroom and slipped into her familiar gray dress, which was still covered in mud.

*   *   *   *   *

That night at the family dinner table, Jasmine had just come in to bring some more green beans when the president made an announcement. "I think it's time to educate Payne in the ways of other countries," he began. "I've arranged for him to go to Russia and be under the watchful eye of John Quincy Adams. There are important peace talks going on."

"But it's so far . . ." Dolley sighed.

Annie looked at Jasmine's face. The smile on it was as wide as a quarter moon.

Payne put down his spoon, and said, "I think I'm still needed here. If there's a war, I don't want to leave the country. I'll stay with my dear mother while you are so busy." He beamed a smile at Dolley, sure she would talk his stepfather out of the Russia idea.

The president seemed to ignore him for a moment, and Jasmine left the room. Then he dug into his coat pocket and pulled out the tin of rouge. "Here, my dear," he said to Dolley. "I've found the tin of rouge you've been looking for." He slid the tin across the table. Dolley picked it up and smiled with delight.

Annie saw the glance exchanged by Payne and James Madison. In a second, Payne realized his Indian costume had been found. He understood the reason he was to go to Russia. Annie sighed when Payne gave up the fight.

"On second thought," Payne said, "perhaps I can be more help if I go to Russia. Those peace talks sound very important. They could stop the war."

The president nodded. "Yes. We do want to be at peace if at all possible, don't we?" he said.

Only Annie and Payne knew that the president

was talking about world peace *and* family peace. *Even though he's not a Quaker,* Annie thought, *I know he'll try hard to keep us out of war, if it's up to him.*

"Well," said Dolley, "if he's going to go, then we must have a party for him before he leaves. I shall need a new dress and turban. Payne will need some new clothes too. And Annie . . ."

"Oh," said Annie, "I'm fine with my Quaker dress. I've decided I'd rather look like a soft gray dove than a parrot."

Her uncle added, "Yes. Doves are the symbol of peace. And I think that fits Annie just fine."

Did You Know?

Anna (or Annie) Payne became Dolley Madison's companion during Mrs. Madison's later life. Dolley adopted Annie as her own daughter, and the two moved back to Washington, D.C. some years after James Madison died. While the events of this story did not happen, many of the details are true, including:

• Lucy Washington married Supreme Court Justice Thomas Todd on Easter Sunday, March 29, 1812.

• In March 1812, Vice President George Clinton was dying.

• War with England was coming quickly. The United States declared war on June 8, 1812.

• Dolley Madison grew up a Quaker. After she married James Madison she left the Quakers. She was known for wearing bright colors and elaborate turbans. She also had a remarkable gift for making people feel welcome at the President's House.

• Payne Todd did give his mother a macaw as a gift. Throughout his life, he gambled away any money he could get. He landed in debtor's prison many times. James Madison paid off his stepson's debts whenever possible, often without telling Dolley. Payne's money troubles caused his mother to be very poor in her old age. Only by selling her husband's papers to Congress did she have enough money to live on.

• James Madison always wore plain, dark suits. He often worked through the night.

• On their wedding day, James gave Dolley a strand of pearls.

• The Freemans were a family of servants who worked at the President's House. (Jasmine's character is fictional.)

• Dolley Madison most likely lied about her age and wore rouge.

• Sukey was Dolley Madison's personal maid.

• In 1813 Payne Todd went to Russia as a secretary. He was treated like royalty and got into debt again.

• After a group of Indians had dined at the President's House, one got lost on the way out. He showed up in Dolley's bedroom, tomahawk raised. She quietly and quickly escorted him out.

• When one of Dolley's nieces visited the President's House, an Indian came up to her on the front lawn and pretended he was going to cut off her curls.